D1455986

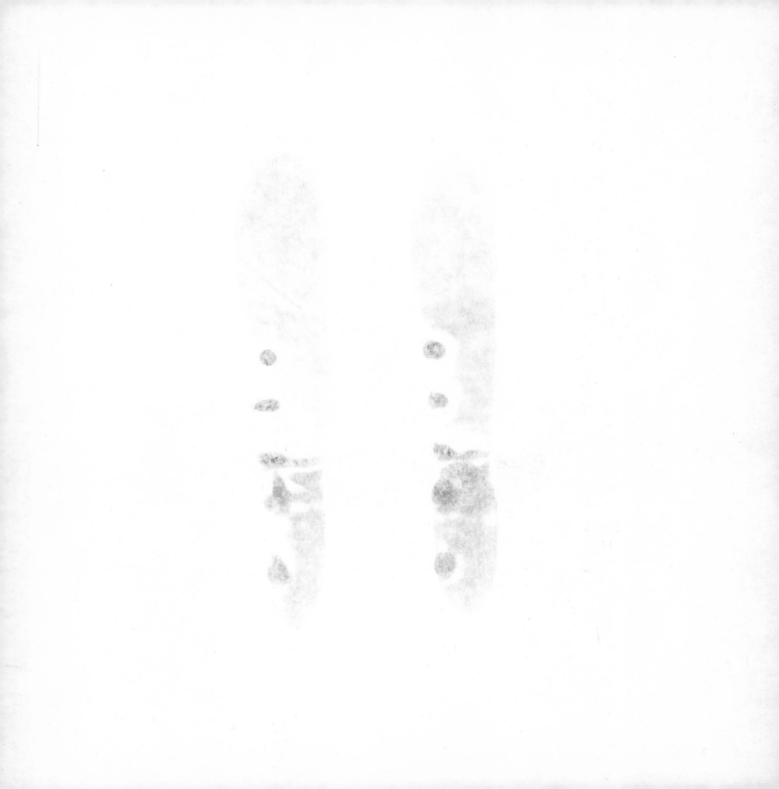

# SPOT A CAT

**A DORLING KINDERSLEY BOOK**

*For Annabel*

First published in Great Britain in 1995
by Dorling Kindersley Limited,
9 Henrietta Street, London, WC2E 8PS

A CIP catalogue record for this book is
available from the British Library.

ISBN 0-7513-5336-1

Colour reproduction by G.R.B. Graphica, Verona
Printed in Italy by L.E.G.O.

# SPOT A CAT

## Selected by Lucy Micklethwait

DORLING KINDERSLEY
LONDON • NEW YORK • STUTTGART

I can see
a big cat.

*Woman with a Cat* Auguste Renoir

# Where is the little cat?

*Night Café at Arles*  Paul Gauguin

Do you see
the scared cat?

*The Annunciation*  Lorenzo Lotto

# Can you
# spot a cat?

*Zoological Garden*  Paul Klee

# This cat is a happy cat.

*Night Rain and Thunder* Utagawa Kuniyoshi

# This cat is a cautious cat.

*Perspective View Down a Corridor*  Samuel van Hoogstraten

# This one is
# a crazy cat.

*Cat* Karel Appel

# Can you spot a cat?

*Christmas Eve: 1951* Patrick Heron

I can see a
white cat.

*Mr. and Mrs. Clark and Percy*  David Hockney

# Can you see
# a black cat?

*Three Women*  Fernand Léger

# Let's find a ginger cat.

*A Princess Watching a Maid Kill a Snake*  Mir Kalan Khan

# Can you spot a cat?

*The Adoration of the Magi*  Jan Brueghel

Here there is a strange cat,
And a sort of flappy bat,
But let's find a face
and a foot with five toes.
Do you see the odd dog?
Can you spot the funny frog?
What shall we find … who knows?

*Dutch Interior I*   Joan Miró

# Picture List

**I can see a big cat.**
Auguste Renoir 1841-1919, French
*Woman with a Cat* c.1875
oil on canvas
56 x 46.4 cm
National Gallery of Art, Washington
Gift of Mr. and Mrs. Benjamin E. Levy

**Where is the little cat?**
Paul Gauguin 1848-1903, French
*Night Café at Arles* 1888
oil on canvas
72 x 92 cm
Pushkin State Museum of Fine
Arts, Moscow

**Do you see the scared cat?**
Lorenzo Lotto c.1480-1556, Italian
*The Annunciation* c.1527
oil on canvas
166 x 114 cm
Pinacoteca Civica, Recanati

**Can you spot a cat?**
Paul Klee 1879-1940, Swiss
*Zoological Garden* 1918
watercolour
17.1 x 23.1 cm
Kunstmuseum, Bern

**This cat is a happy cat.**
Utagawa Kuniyoshi 1797-1861,
Japanese
*Night Rain and Thunder* from the series
*Beauties and Episodes of Ōtsu-e*
early 1850s
woodblock fan print
21 x 29 cm (image size)
Victoria and Albert Museum, London

**This cat is a cautious cat.**
Samuel van Hoogstraten
1627-1678, Dutch
*Perspective View Down
a Corridor* 1662
oil on canvas
260 x 136 cm
Dyrham Park, Avon

**This one is a crazy cat.**
Karel Appel b. 1921, Dutch
*Cat* 1971
oil and papier-mâché on canvas
89 x 116 cm
Private Collection

**Can you spot a cat?**
Patrick Heron b. 1920, British
*Christmas Eve: 1951*
oil on canvas
182.8 x 304.8 cm
Private Collection

**I can see a white cat.**
David Hockney b. 1937, British
*Mr. and Mrs. Clark and Percy* 1970-71
acrylic on canvas
213.4 x 304.8 cm
Tate Gallery, London

**Can you see a black cat?**
Fernand Léger 1881-1955, French
*Three Women* 1921
oil on canvas
183.5 x 251.5 cm
Museum of Modern Art, New York
Mrs. Simon Guggenheim Fund

**Let's find a ginger cat.**
Mir Kalan Khan, Indian
*A Princess Watching a Maid Kill
a Snake* c.1770
gouache on paper
21.3 x 16.8 cm
British Library, London

**Can you spot a cat?**
Jan Brueghel 1568-1625, Flemish
*The Adoration of the Magi* 1598
body colour on vellum
32.9 x 47.9 cm
National Gallery, London

**Here there is a strange cat, …**
Joan Miró 1893-1983, Spanish
*Dutch Interior I* 1928
oil on canvas
91.8 x 73 cm
Museum of Modern Art, New York
Mrs. Simon Guggenheim Fund

**Front Cover**
*Woman with a Cat* (detail),
Auguste Renoir
**Spine**
*Perspective View Down a Corridor*
(detail), Samuel van Hoogstraten
**Half-title page**
*Zoological Garden* (detail), Paul Klee

**Imprint page**
*Night Rain and Thunder* (detail),
Utagawa Kuniyoshi
**Title page**
*Mr. and Mrs. Clark and Percy,*
David Hockney
**Picture List**
*The Annunciation* (detail), Lorenzo Lotto
*Dutch Interior I* (detail), Joan Miró

# Acknowledgments

The publisher would like to thank the
following for their kind permission to
reproduce the photographs:

*Night Café at Arles*, Bridgeman Art Library / Pushkin
State Museum of Fine Arts: **7**
*A Princess Watching a Maid Kill a Snake*, The British
Library / Oriental and India Office Collections: **25**
*Cat,* Christies Images: **17**
*Christmas Eve: 1951*, © 1995 Patrick Heron All rights
reserved. DACS: **19**
*Zoological Garden,* Kunstmuseum, Bern, © DACS 1995:
**1 (detail), 11**
*Three Women (Le Grand Déjeuner)*, © 1995 The
Museum of Modern Art, New York, © DACS 1995: **23**
*Dutch Interior I* , © 1995 The Museum of Modern Art,
New York, © ADAGP Paris and DACS London 1995:
**29, 31 (detail)**

*Woman with a Cat,* © 1994 Board of Trustees, National
Gallery of Art, Washington: **front cover (detail), 5**
*The Adoration of the Magi,* The National Gallery,
London: **27**
*Perspective View Down a Corridor*, The National Trust /
Derrick E. Witty: **spine (detail), 15**
*The Annunciation*, SCALA / Recanati, Museo Civica:
**9, 30 (detail)**
*Mr. and Mrs. Clark and Percy*, Tate Gallery, London
© Tradhart Ltd: **3, 21**
*Night Rain and Thunder*, Victoria and Albert Museum,
London: **2 (detail), 13**